LOOK OUT FOR MORE STORIES OF MAYHEM AND CHAOS IN

VULGAR THE VIKING AND THE GREAT GULP GAMES

VULGAR THE VIKING AND THE SPOOKY SCHOOL TRIP

VULGAR THE VIKING IN BLUBBER'S GOT TALENT!

VULGAR THE VIKING AND THE ROCK CAKE RAIDERS

ILLUSTRATED BY
SARAH HORNE

nosy crow

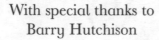

With special thanks to
Barry Hutchison

First published in the UK in 2012 by Nosy Crow
The Crow's Nest, 10a Lant St
London, SE1 1QR, UK

Nosy Crow and associated logos are trademarks and/or
registered trademarks of Nosy Crow Ltd

Text © Hothouse Fiction, 2012
Illustrations © Sarah Horne, 2012

The right of Hothouse Fiction and Sarah Horne to be identified as the author
and illustrator respectively of this work has been asserted by them in accordance
with the Copyright, Designs and Patents Act 1988.

A CIP catalogue record for this book will be available from the British Library

Printed and bound in the UK by Clays Ltd, St Ives Plc

Papers used by Nosy Crow are made from wood grown in sustainable forests.

ISBN: 978 0 85763 056 8

www.nosycrow.com

CHAPTER ONE

AN EARLY START

COCK-A-DOODLE-DOOOOOO!

The cockerel's cry tore through the early morning air.

In a messy bedroom, in a small hut, somewhere near the centre of the sleepy town of Blubber, a young boy named Vulgar threw back his covers and leapt out of bed.

His covers gave a loud, grumpy *woof* as

 1

they landed in a heap on the floor.

"Sorry, Grunt," said Vulgar, looking down at the shaggy dog who had been sleeping on his legs. "Forgot you were there!"

Grunt gave a low growl of annoyance and scratched his ear with his back leg.

Vulgar smoothed out his leather tunic and tightened the string belt of his seal-skin shorts.

He'd slept in his clothes last night, because today was a big day and he didn't want to waste a moment of it getting dressed.

Vulgar kicked open his bedroom door and hurried along the narrow passageway that led to the kitchen.

As he bounded into the room, Vulgar spotted a huge, dark figure standing in the corner.

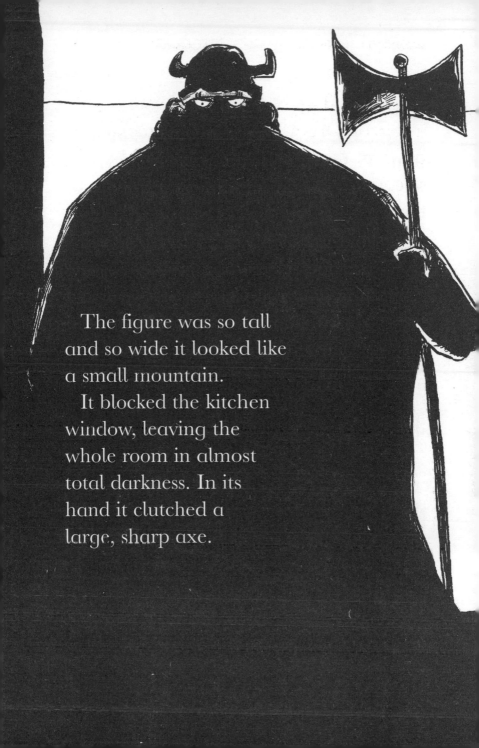

The figure was so tall
and so wide it looked like
a small mountain.

It blocked the kitchen
window, leaving the
whole room in almost
total darkness. In its
hand it clutched a
large, sharp axe.

"Morning, Mum," said Vulgar.

"By Odin's beard!" boomed Vulgar's mum, Helga, her voice making the flames of the fire quiver and shake. "What's got you out of bed so early?"

"It's History Day!" said Vulgar excitedly. Behind him, Grunt padded into the room. The dog gave a snort as he slouched down on to the floor beside the fire, before falling asleep again.

"History Day?" repeated Helga, splitting a log as tall as Vulgar with one blow of her axe.

"I've told you about it a hundred times," said Vulgar. "It's a whole day of learning about Vikings."

Vulgar's mum frowned. "We *are* Vikings," she said.

"No, *proper* Vikings!" cried Vulgar. "Like in the olden days. You know? All looting and plundering and adventure on

4

the high seas." He shook his head sadly. "Not like the Vikings who live in Blubber, all snoozing and gardening and ... and ... *knitting*."

Helga's frown deepened. "Nothing wrong with knitting."

"Yes, there is," groaned Vulgar. "It's *boring*, just like everything else around here. Except History Day."

"I've never seen you this excited about learning stuff before," said Helga. She eyed her son suspiciously. "Are you up to something?"

"No."

"Because you're *usually* up to something."

"I'm not up to anything," Vulgar said, sighing. "It's just ... *it's History Day!* About *real* Vikings." He puffed up his chest and clenched his fists. "Just like I'm going to be."

 5

"Well, Mr Real Viking, before you go anywhere, you can get in the bath and wash that hair of yours. It's filthy."

"But *Mum*," groaned Vulgar. "It's *supposed* to be filthy. Whoever heard of a Viking with clean hair?"

"What about your father?" Helga asked him. "Your father always has clean hair."

"Dad?!" spluttered Vulgar. "Grunt's more of a Viking than he is."

At the sound of his name, Grunt opened one eye, chuffed loudly, then went back to sleep.

"Right, fine," sighed Helga, turning back to the log pile. "But wash your hands before breakfast. You look like you've been juggling elk poo."

Vulgar looked at his hands. His mum was right. Then again, he *had* been juggling elk poo. It was one of his favourite hobbies.

 7

"No way," said Vulgar defiantly. He folded his arms in front of him. "Vikings don't wash their hands. We'd sooner have them cut off."

Helga hefted her axe and stared hard at her son's skinny wrists. "That could be arranged," she growled.

Vulgar gulped. His mum didn't make idle threats. She'd once dangled him upside down from the window for refusing to cut his toenails.

She'd strapped him to a boulder and rolled it down a hill when he'd refused to eat his sprouts. But surely even she wouldn't go as far as chopping his hands off?

Would she?

"OK," he grumbled at last. "I'll wash my hands. But just this once."

Helga lowered the axe. The corners of her mouth curved into a smile. "Wise move," she said, turning back to the log pile.

Stepping over the sleeping Grunt, Vulgar approached the large wooden basin the family used for washing. Everything got washed in the basin, from faces to clothes to dirty dishes. By the end of the day, the water would be a dark, murky grey, but at this time in the morning it was crystal clear.

Please, thought Vulgar, as he drew closer to the basin, *let today be the day...*

Taking a deep breath, Vulgar stretched on to his tiptoes and looked at his reflection, shimmering on the water's surface.

Thor's bum-fluff, he thought, staring crossly at his smooth, hairless chin. *Still no beard.*

Vulgar wanted many things in life. He wanted a broadsword with a skull for a handle. He wanted a shield made of solid gold and silver. And he wanted to be

10

strong enough to lift both of them
without falling over.

More than anything, though, Vulgar wanted a beard. And not just any beard. He wanted a *proper* beard, like proper Vikings used to have. A big, red beard that forked into two at the bottom, like a horned helmet for his chin.

He waggled his fingers in the water, chasing his reflection away. No beard today. Maybe tomorrow.

Vulgar turned back into the kitchen. A lump of mouldy cheese and a hunk of stale bread lay on the table.

"Breakfast," said his mum. "Get it while it's ... there."

Vulgar pounced on the food, snatching it up before the mice could whisk it away. As he was shoving it into his mouth, the door opened and a skinny man with very clean hair shuffled inside.

"Morning, son. Morning, wife," said Harald, Vulgar's dad. He stretched up to his full height and tried to plant a kiss on Helga's cheek. Being far too short to reach, he only managed to kiss her elbow, but they both seemed happy with that.

"How were the toilets this morning?" asked Helga, returning to her work.

Harald shuddered. "Ooh, they were proper blocked," he said. "Up to my elbows I was, trying to get them unclogged."

Crossing to the basin, Harald dipped his arms in the water. It immediately turned a murky shade of brown.

 13

"You're awake early," he said to Vulgar. "Are you up to something?"

"No!"

"Because you're *usually* up to something."

"That's what *I* said," Helga told him.

"I'm not up to anything!" insisted Vulgar. "It's History Day today. When we learn about proper Vikings."

Harald dried his hands on his thin, wispy beard, then wrung them together nervously. "What, plundering and adventuring and stuff like that?"

"Exactly!"

"I tried it once," said Harald. "Not my cup of tea. All those big waves. I get seasick just doing the washing-up, don't I, dearest?"

"That's your usual excuse," grunted Helga, not looking round.

"You don't want to bother with all that

old-fashioned stuff," said Harald, with a wave of a brown-stained hand. "You want to get a proper job. Like me."

"Cleaning toilets?" spluttered Vulgar. "That's not a—"

"Vuuuuuuulgaaaaaaaar!"

The shout came from outside, stopping Vulgar mid-sentence.

"Knut's here," said Vulgar, cramming the last of the bread in his mouth.

"Coming!" he cried to his best friend, spraying crumbs all over the kitchen table. "Grunt! Walkies!"

At the sound of the word, Grunt's ear twitched, and the shaggy old dog leapt bolt upright.

Still chewing, Vulgar grabbed his cloak and helmet from the peg on the wall, threw open the back door and bolted out into the garden, not bothering to say goodbye.

15

This was it.
History Day had finally begun!

CHAPTER TWO

THE GREAT HALL

Vulgar and Grunt dashed along the path and cleared the garden gate in a single leap. Vulgar's best friend, Knut Knutson, stood on the dirt track that ran past the hut. He was almost a whole foot taller than Vulgar, even though they were both eight, but Knut always slouched so the boys looked almost the same height.

Knut didn't have a beard either. In fact, he looked even less like a proper

Viking than Vulgar did. For a start, he was far too skinny. Proper Vikings needed to be broad-shouldered, with chests like rum barrels. Knut looked like a garden rake, with a turnip on top for a head. Even his helmet looked wrong. It was much too big. And Knut had accidentally broken off one of the horns. He'd stuck it back on, but because he wasn't paying attention – Knut hardly ever paid attention – he'd put it back the wrong way up. Now one horn curved upwards, and one horn curved down. It made

18

Knut look like he had a giant letter "Z" stuck through his head.

"History Day!" announced Vulgar. "Excited?"

Knut shrugged. "S'pose."

They hurried off in the direction of the Great Hall, with Grunt trotting along behind them.

"I wonder if there'll be demonstrations," said Vulgar.

"Demonstrations of what?" asked Knut.

"You know – proper Viking stuff. Like ... like ... pillaging!"

Knut considered this. "What exactly *is* pillaging?"

"Well," began Vulgar, waving his hand about vaguely. "It's like ... um ... it's a bit like stealing. Only more, er..."

"More pillagey?"

"Exactly!"

"Here, Vulgar," said Knut, "maybe

19

they'll pillage us?"

Vulgar stopped in the middle of the dirt track, his eyes suddenly wide. "That. Would. Be. *Brilliant!*"

He hurried on, moving even faster than before. The track took them through the town, past old women weaving on their front steps, past younger women scrubbing moss from the wooden walls of their thatched huts, and past men of all ages tending their rock gardens.

"Look at that lot," muttered Vulgar. "Weaving. Cleaning. Growing vegetables." He shook his head in disgust. "I mean ... *vegetables!*"

"Someone's got to grow vegetables," said Knut.

"Yes, but not *us!*" exclaimed Vulgar. "Not *Vikings!* We should be sailing to other countries and taking all *their* vegetables, not growing our own!"

Knut gave another shrug. They hurried on for a few more minutes, not even slowing down to admire the view of the snow-capped mountains across the fjord.

Finally, they arrived at the Great Hall – the huge building in the centre of Blubber. It was twice as tall as any of the huts around it, with life-size polar bears carved on to each corner. Grunt took one

look at the steep steps leading up to the doors, slumped to the ground and started snoring.

"Come on," Vulgar said to Knut. "We don't want to be late."

Inside, the Great Hall looked even greater than usual. Banners had been draped between the massive wooden pillars that held up the roof. A huge fire crackled in the hearth.

The ceremonial weapons were all polished and gleaming. Long tapestries hung on the walls, depicting great battles of old. And the room was full of Viking children, all chattering excitedly about History Day.

Only one girl was not talking with the others. Princess Freya Gold-Hair, the only daughter of King Olaf, sat on a padded chair with her back resting against one of the pillars.

"Wotcha, Freya," said Vulgar cheerily.

Freya's delicate nose wrinkled, as if detecting an unpleasant smell. She turned her head, deliberately looking away from Vulgar and Knut.

"Helloooo!" said Vulgar, leaning around so Freya had no choice but to look at him. She met his eyes briefly, then turned away again.

"Oh, I'm sorry," said Vulgar, grinning. "I forgot you don't talk to us commoners." He gave an exaggerated bow. "Forgive me, your high and mightiness."

With that, Vulgar turned and scurried away. He'd only gone a few paces, though, when he stopped and tiptoed back towards the princess.

"Watch this," he mouthed silently, grinning at Knut.

Knut covered his mouth with his hands

 24

to stop himself laughing as Vulgar gently took hold of Freya's long, blonde pigtails, one in each hand. Slowly, carefully, he drew them around the pillar behind Freya and tied them together in a big knot.

He had just finished when Freya felt her hair being messed with.

"Hey!" she cried, standing up. She stepped forward. "What do you think you're— *Ow!*"

Vulgar and Knut erupted into gales of laughter as Freya's hair yanked her back. She gave another cry of pain as she fell back down on to the seat.

"I'll get you for this," she hissed, reaching behind her and working furiously to untie the knot. "Just you wait!"

Before Vulgar could reply, a frail-looking man, bent and crooked with age, hobbled into the hall, waving his walking-stick in the air.

"Right, quieten down, you lot," snapped Harrumf, the steward of the Great Hall. "We ain't got all day."

The chatter of the children gradually

fell away into silence. Harrumf banged his stick on the wooden floor three times. *Thock! Thock! Thock!*

"All rise," he cried, "for 'is Most Majestic of Majesties. The greatest warrior wot Blubber 'as ever seen. The man wot put the *king* into *Viking...*"

Harrumf ran out of breath at that point, and had to stop to gulp down more air. He coughed loudly before continuing. "The one ... the only ... the flippin' marvellous ... Kiiiiiiing Olaf the Unstoppable!"

The children who were already standing stood to attention. Even Knut's slouch didn't look quite so slouchy. The children who had been sitting leapt to their feet. Only Freya remained seated. She glared at Vulgar, still struggling to untie her hair. Vulgar gave her a friendly wave, just as the bulging stomach of

27

King Olaf
appeared
through the
doorway at
the back of the
hall, closely
followed by
the rest
of him.

28

The crowd of children began to whoop and cheer.

"Thank you, thank you," muttered the king, swallowing down the last bite of a turkey drumstick. Tossing the bone over his shoulder, he gave a loud burp, then wiped his greasy fingers on his enormous red beard.

29

"Be seated," he announced, in a voice that shook the walls, "and listen closely, for I am about to tell you tales so terrible and terrifying, they'll make your eyes burst open and drip down your face!"

Vulgar's mouth stretched into a wide, toothy grin.

Now this, he thought, *is more like it!*

CHAPTER THREE

A TALL TALE

A hushed silence fell over the audience as they settled down to listen to King Olaf. Vulgar leaned forward and held his head up, not wanting to miss a single word of what was about to be said.

"BOGIES!" roared King Olaf, in a voice that made everyone in the front three rows jump. Vulgar blinked. He hadn't been expecting bogies.

"That's all I had to eat," the king

continued. "Gooey, sticky
bogies from the darkest
corners of my royal
nostrils."

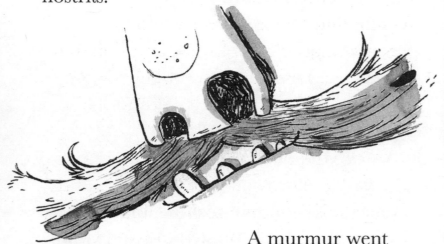

A murmur went
through the crowd.
Clearly it hadn't been
expecting bogies either.

"I'd been adrift at sea for months, my
loyal crew either killed in battle or lost
beneath the waves. My food supply was
long gone, knocked overboard during
a fight with a crazed sea serpent that

I eventually managed to slay with just these bare hands."

King Olaf held his pudgy hands up for the audience to admire, before continuing. "Lesser men would have given up, gone mad from starvation and loneliness. Lesser men would have gone crying and wailing to the gods for help. But I am not a lesser man."

"What did you do?" asked Vulgar, fascinated. Harrumf raised his stick and opened his mouth to scold Vulgar for interrupting, but King Olaf spoke before the old man got the chance.

"Excellent question, my boy," said the king. "I knew I had to find food, and fast. So I climbed the mast and scanned the horizon. For days I stayed up there, drinking seagulls' blood and eating bogies. And then one day, just like that, there it was."

"There *what* was?" breathed Vulgar.

"Land, my boy. Land! An island, in fact. I set the sail and soon arrived on the coast. Their army was vast, but no match for a true Viking warrior like me. I defeated them, all five thousand soldiers. It wasn't easy, mind you – took me almost an hour – but when the last man was beaten, I looted every single one of their huts."

"Did you pillage them as well?" asked Vulgar, bouncing up and down with excitement.

"You bet your broadsword I did!" said Olaf proudly. "I looted *and* pillaged them good and proper, took all their food back to my longship, and set sail for home."

"And did you ransack them?"

"Yes. I looted and pillaged and ransacked all ten thousand of them," said the king.

"I thought you said there were *five* thousand soldiers?" said Knut.

King Olaf frowned. "Um..."

"Where was the island?" asked Vulgar, desperate for every last detail.

King Olaf frowned a bit more. "Er ... I ... can't remember."

"You must remember!" said Vulgar. "Vikings never forget the places they've conquered."

"What? I mean, yes, of course." Olaf rubbed at his beard. "It's ... um ... nowhere," he said. "I, er, set it on fire and it sank into the sea, and, er, no one survived."

"You sank a whole island?" gasped Vulgar. "That's *amazing*."

"Yes, well ... I'm an amazing man," said the king. "So, anyway, we set sail—"

"Weren't all your crew dead?" asked Vulgar.

"Er, yes, *I* set sail—"

"I would've eaten the seagulls," said Knut suddenly. Everyone in the hall turned to look at him.

"What?" asked King Olaf, looking flustered. "What seagulls?"

"The ones whose blood you were drinking," Knut said with a shrug. "I'd have probably just eaten them, instead of

 37

the bogies."

"Or taken it in turns?" suggested Vulgar. "Seagull, bogey, seagull, bogey?"

Olaf looked from Vulgar to Knut and back again. His mouth was hanging open, but no words came out.

"Or I'd have waited until a seagull caught a fish, then I'd have eaten that," said Knut. "Seagulls are quite good at catching fish."

"Tell us how you beat the army! Did they all attack you at once or one at a time?" asked Vulgar, who cared more about the fighting than the food. He was getting excited just at the thought of the battle. "Did you chop their knees off? I'd have chopped their knees off, even though my mum says that's not playing fair."

"Vikings don't play fair," Knut reminded him.

"Exactly!" cried Vulgar. He fixed his gaze on King Olaf. "Have you chopped anyone's knees off? Tell us what it's like!"

"Well, yes, I chopped off the, er, sea monster's knees," said King Olaf. He looked a lot less confident now, and his face was turning the same shade of red as his beard.

39

"But you said you fought him with your bare hands," said Vulgar, frowning.

"And you said it was a sea serpent," said Knut. "They don't have knees."

"What colour was its blood?" asked Vulgar.

"Er, yes, well, I'd love to tell you," mumbled the king. "But I've just remembered that I have to go ... somewhere else. Right now."

"But what about History Day?" asked Vulgar.

"Come back next year," replied Olaf, waddling towards the front of the hall.

"Bye for now!" the king called as he
squeezed his huge
bulk
through
the
doors.
For a few
minutes, no one
moved. Then Harrumpf
banged his stick on the floor
and bellowed, "Right you
lot, no 'angin about in 'ere.
The basket-weavin' workshop
is startin' now."
One by one, the children got
to their feet and followed him
out. None of them were quite sure
why King Olaf had gone running
off, but they were all agreed on one
thing: History Day had been a big
let-down.

Or rather, they were *almost* all agreed.

"That. Was. *Brilliant!*" cried Vulgar. He hadn't moved from his spot on the floor. Besides him and Knut, there were only a handful of children left in the hall.

"That's what proper Vikings are about – sea serpents and battles."

"And bogies," Knut reminded him.

"Yeah! And bogies," said Vulgar, grinning.

Knut sniffed. "It was a bit shorter than I expected," he said. "Not really 'History Day'. More like 'History Five Minutes'."

"But *what a five minutes!*" said Vulgar, sighing happily.

"What do you want to do now?" asked Knut.

"Well, I'm *not* doing basket-weaving," said Vulgar.

"I've got my pocket money. We could go buy some cakes from Ivar the Baker," suggested Knut.

Vulgar jumped to his feet. "Buy cakes?" he scoffed. "*Buy* cakes?! Vikings don't *buy* cakes – we *pillage* them!"

Knut didn't look convinced. "Can you pillage a cake?"

"You can pillage anything if you try hard enough," Vulgar told him. He was hopping from foot to foot. "Ivar's shop is on the other side of the fishpond," he said. "We should sail across it in our longboat, pillage the cakes, then sail back here and eat them."

"Um, we don't have a longboat," Knut reminded him.

"Loki's kneecaps!" cursed Vulgar, punching his fist against his palm. "You're right."

He thought for a moment, then clicked his fingers. "But wait! We're in the Great Hall. They keep all the building supplies in the cellar. Nails. Wood. Things like that. I bet there's even cloth for a sail. We can *build* our own longboat!"

Knut's face turned several shades paler. "The cellar?" he whispered. "I heard there are trolls down there."

Vulgar grinned. Grabbing Knut by the arm, he darted past the few

remaining children, ducked into a corner, and *creaked* open the thick

wooden
door that led
to the cellar steps. "If
there are trolls," he said,
"they'd better stay out of our
way!"

The stone stairs leading down into the Great Hall's cellar were dark and narrow. What little light snuck in through the open door soon faded as the two boys crept down the steps.

"Are you s-s-sure about this?" asked Knut, sticking close to Vulgar as they finally reached the bottom.

"It's just the door," said Vulgar. "Stop being scared, Vikings don't get—"

"*Ssssh!*" hissed Knut. "Listen!"

Vulgar stopped talking, and that was when he heard it. The slow *clop-clop-clop* of footsteps on the stairs behind them. Something was with them in the cellar. Something was moving in the shadows.

And whatever it was, it was getting closer.

 46

CHAPTER FOUR

THE THING IN THE CELLAR

"It's a troll!" screamed Knut. "Or a dragon! Or ... or a *dragon troll*!"

"Shut up!" hissed Vulgar, clamping a hand over Knut's mouth. He was too late, though. Whatever was coming down the stairs had heard them, and now it was moving faster, clomping down the steps, closer and closer and—

"Hello," said a voice from somewhere right behind them. This time both boys screamed, before Vulgar recognised the voice.

"Freya?" he groaned. "What are you doing here?"

A candle spluttered to life, and lit up the princess's face. "I would ask you the same thing," she said, "but I know exactly what you're doing here. I heard you talking upstairs."

Vulgar shot Knut a nervous glance. "What did you hear, exactly?"

A sly smile spread across Freya's face. "*Everything*," she said. "The pond. The cakes. Building your own longboat. I heard it all, and I'm going to tell your mum you skipped basket-weaving. Unless..."

"Unless what?" demanded Vulgar.

"Unless you let me play, too," she replied.

Vulgar looked horrified. "Play?" he

said. "*Play?* We're not playing, we're looting!"

"And pillaging," Knut reminded him.

"Yeah, and pillaging," agreed Vulgar. "We're *proper* looting and *proper* pillaging, like *proper* Vikings do. It's not a game!"

"Look," snapped Freya, bringing her face close to his. "If you don't let me join in, I'll tell my father what you're up to, *and* that you tied my hair to the pillar. You'll be thrown in the dungeon. What do you think of that?"

"But girls can't be Viking warriors," said Vulgar weakly. He didn't really fancy the dungeons much. He'd heard there was a machine down there that ripped your beard out,

49

one hair at a time. Vulgar didn't have a beard, but he still didn't like the sound of it.

"They can now," sniffed Freya, and she pushed past them into the cellar.

"Well, you showed her," said Knut, trying his best not to laugh. "Some Viking warrior, being pushed around by a girl."

"Yeah, well at least I don't scream like one," replied Vulgar, before he stomped after Freya.

It took a few minutes to light the torches around the cellar, but just a few seconds to realise that building a longboat was going to be more difficult than they had thought.

Vulgar had expected to find enough supplies for a whole fleet of ships. It turned out that he had been wrong.

"So," he said, "tell me again what we've got."

Knut looked down at the items laid out on the floor before him. He took a deep breath. "One barrel, full of ale; three planks of wood, all broken; a big rock; another rock, not quite so big as the other one; something green and squidgy." He bent down and gave it a sniff. "I think it might have been cheese, but I'm not sure. And two oars, different sizes. That's the lot."

"Building a longboat out of this stuff isn't going to be easy," said Vulgar.

"Building *anything* out of this stuff isn't going to be easy," corrected Freya. She sighed. "This is a complete waste of time."

"Where's your Viking spirit?" cried Vulgar. He stared accusingly at the princess. "When your dad was lost at sea, did he give up? No! He made do with what he had. He ate bogies and drank seagulls' blood! And that's what we're going to do."

"What, eat bogies?" asked Knut, with a frown.

"I'll do no such thing," gasped Freya. "Princesses do *not* eat bogies."

"No, I mean we're going to make do with what we've got," explained Vulgar. "See, look at this!"

With a heave, Vulgar tipped the barrel over. Gallons of ale sloshed out on to the floor. When it was empty, he hoisted the barrel back up and peered inside. "I bet we could fit in there," he said. "And it's watertight, too."

"How do you know?" asked Knut.

"Well, if it can keep beer in, it can keep water out," said Vulgar. He looked around the cellar. The rocks would be no help, and the squidgy green stuff was no good. He couldn't think of any uses for the broken planks, either, so that left only the oars.

He grabbed the longest oar and propped it up inside the barrel, so the flat

 54

end was raised towards the ceiling. "This could be our mast. We can tie my cloak on for a sail!"

"We're hardly going to sail very far like that, are we?" scoffed Freya.

"We won't have to," said Vulgar. He could see his whole plan coming together now. "We've still got one oar, so we can row across the pond."

Freya pulled a face, and Vulgar thought she was about to object. He was surprised when she said, "It might work. I suppose."

"Of course it'll work!" cried Vulgar.

Over the next ten minutes, Vulgar shouted enthusiastic instructions to the other two, using everything he knew about constructing a longboat. Which was precisely nothing.

"Doesn't it need, like, a dragon's head at the front?" asked Knut, halfway

 55

through putting the boat together.

Vulgar immediately set to work on one of the broken planks, carving it into the shape of the scariest face he could think of.

"Here, that looks quite like your mum," said Knut, when the carving was finished.

"Yeah," said Vulgar, hooking the terrifying figurehead on to the side of the barrel. "I know!"

 57

At last, it was finished. Vulgar and the others stepped back to admire their handiwork.

"It's not really a *long*boat, is it?" said Freya.

"More a shortboat," agreed Knut.

"Well, more like a barrel with a stick in it," continued the princess.

"It's perfect!" Vulgar told them. "Grab an end and help me carry it up to the pond." He rubbed his hands together in anticipation as his crew followed his orders. His very first Viking adventure was about to set sail!

CHAPTER FIVE

THE GREAT CROSSING

SPLASH!

The barrel-boat bobbed violently as the three would-be pillagers dropped it into the pond. For a moment, it looked like it might sink straight to the bottom, but it rose up again just before water started sloshing in over the sides.

The children leaned over the little wooden dock by the side of the pond and peered down at their vessel.

"It's heavier than it looks," said Vulgar, rubbing his aching arms.

"I bet even real longboats aren't that heavy," agreed Freya. "I bet it's your mum's big face that made it weigh so much."

"Hey, leave my mum's face out of it!" Vulgar warned her. "It'll scare away any sea monsters we meet."

"Pond monsters," Knut reminded him.

"Same thing," shrugged Vulgar. "Ponds are where sea monsters go on holiday."

With a well-timed jump, Vulgar landed inside the barrel.

"What happened to *ladies first*?" Freya asked him.

"I keep telling you, you don't get lady Vikings, so I'm just going to pretend you're a boy."

"Don't you dare," snarled Freya.

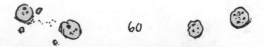

She hopped into the barrel next to
Vulgar. It spun wildly and, for a
moment, they forgot their argument and
raised their arms above their heads,
laughing as the barrel twirled them
round and round.

"Come on, Knut," urged Vulgar, when
the spinning slowed to a stop. "Hurry
up."

Vulgar couldn't wait to set sail. Ivar's
rock cakes were legendary, and they
were just across the water. Not only did
they taste delicious but they could knock
a man out from twenty paces, if you
threw them hard enough. This, for
Vulgar, was the sign of a truly great
cake.

"Here I come!" cried Knut.

There was a loud *thud*, and Knut
landed in the barrel, head first. His legs
kicked wildly in thin air for a moment

61

before he managed to turn himself the right way up.

It was a tight squeeze with all of them in there, and the barrel was very low in the water. Freya was saying, "It's a good job there's no one else coming with us," when a dog hit her squarely in the face.

"There you are, Grunt," laughed
Vulgar, as his dog licked Freya's face
then squeezed into the tiny gap between
Vulgar's feet. "Right, Knut, get rowing!"

Knut grumbled as Vulgar pushed the
oar into his hand. "Don't see why I have
to row."

"Because I'm the captain," Vulgar told him. Knut pushed the oar into the water and paddled. The barrel turned in a complete circle.

"No, *I'm* the captain," said Freya. Knut dipped the oar into the water on the opposite side of the barrel, and it began to spin the other way.

"You don't get girl captains!"

"Yes, but you're pretending I'm a boy, and this *boy* says he's captain. Because, might I remind you, this *boy* is a princess!"

Knut paddled left, then paddled right. The barrel moved in a reasonably straight line.

"Boys can't be princesses!"

"But boys can be captains," said Freya.

Vulgar frowned. He had a horrible feeling he was walking into a trap. "Well, yeah..."

"Good. Then I'll be captain," said Freya, and she crossed her arms to signal that the argument was over. "Start rowing, Knut," she commanded, before she realised that he already had, and that they were almost at the opposite shore.

"What's the plan, captain?" asked Knut. He was careful not to look at

65

anyone when he said it.

"Me and Freya jump ashore, loot and plunder some cakes..." began Vulgar.

"And pillage," Knut reminded him.

"Oh, yeah, and pillage," agreed Vulgar. "We loot, plunder *and* pillage the cakes, get back to the longboat..."

"Shortboat," corrected Knut.

"Barrel," said Freya.

"Whatever," sighed Vulgar. "We get back here, where you'll be waiting to row us back, and Thor's your uncle – mission complete."

"That's a stupid plan," snorted Freya. "It's so obvious. You'll be caught right away."

The barrel bumped against the shore. Freya and Vulgar leapt out. Knut and Grunt stayed behind. "You need a distraction," said the princess.

"Like what?"

66

Freya's scream was so high-pitched it could have made a troll's head burst.

Startled, Vulgar looked along the shoreline to where a row of rickety wooden huts stood. People came rushing outside to find out what the fuss was all about.

At the far end of the row of huts, a fat man with a bald head and a pasty white face appeared in a doorway. Vulgar recognised Ivar right away. The big baker waddled in the direction of Freya's screams.

"What are you doing? Ivar's coming over!" whispered Vulgar.

"That's the point," Freya told him, pausing to catch her breath. "Now hurry up, I can't stand here screaming all day."

As Freya let out another screech, Vulgar slipped around the back of the huts and hurried along to the end of the row. The aroma of baking drifted from Ivar's hut, drawing Vulgar inside. The young Viking's eyes lit up when he spotted a tray of rock cakes cooling on the table.

The cakes were warm, but not so warm that Vulgar couldn't hold them. He grabbed two in each hand and shoved them down his seal-skin shorts. He snatched another four, and crammed

them up inside his leather
tunic. Another two
went into his boots,
and the last one
he tucked beneath
his horned
helmet.

Vulgar looked down at the empty tray and grinned proudly. "Looted, plundered *and* pillaged," he said, then he turned to the door.

A hulking shape stood in the doorway. In one hand it held a rolling pin. "Well, well, well," growled Ivar, stepping inside the hut. He hit the rolling pin against the palm of his other hand menacingly. "What *have* we got here?"

CHAPTER SIX

THE GREAT ESCAPE

Vulgar thought fast. There was only one
door in and out of the baker's shop, and
Ivar was standing in front of it, blocking
his escape. If Vulgar had a broadsword,
he could have scared the baker off, but
he didn't have a broadsword. He didn't
even have a narrowsword. In fact, he
didn't have any weapons at all.

Except...

Quick as a flash, Vulgar lifted his

helmet and grabbed the rock cake. Ivar's broad face pulled into a scowl.

"Where did you get that?" he demanded. "Give it to me, right now."

"Well ... OK," said Vulgar, taking aim. "You asked for it!"

THONK!

The heavy cake hit Ivar right between the eyes. The baker staggered backwards towards the door, his face suddenly red with fury.

"Please fall over, please fall over, please fall over," whispered Vulgar. But today wasn't his lucky day. Ivar stumbled, but it didn't look like he was going to fall.

At least, he wasn't going to fall until a flea-bitten bundle of fur appeared behind him and flopped down at his feet. As Ivar staggered back, his heels bumped into the furry lump. His arms flailed around wildly for a few seconds before he toppled backwards like a falling tree, and hit the ground with a *thud*.

"Good boy, Grunt!" cried Vulgar, as the furry bundle stood up. Grunt gave a very brief wag of his tail, then picked up the rock cake Vulgar had thrown at the baker. He held the cake in his jaws and looked up at his master.

"It's all yours," Vulgar told him, and the dog swallowed the cake in two gulps. "You earned it!"

"Get back here," roared Ivar, as Vulgar hopped over him and ran, as fast as he could, back to the barrel-boat. Grunt raced along behind, and in no time they reached Freya. She was still on the shore, surrounded by concerned adults, who were trying to find out why she had been screaming.

Vulgar pushed through the crowd and grabbed the princess by the arm.

"What are you doing?" she demanded. "Unhand me!"

"We have to go," said Vulgar.

"You can't tell me what to do—" began Freya, before an angry shout cut her off.

"Thieves! Looters! Plunderers!" cried Ivar, as he stomped towards them, swinging his rolling pin like a club. "I'll roll you in flour and fry up the lot of you!"

Freya swallowed nervously. "We have

to go," she muttered.

"Yeah," agreed Vulgar, dragging Freya towards the shore. "That's what I said."

The crowd began to mutter as Ivar drew closer. "Stop 'em!" he barked. "They're dirty no-good cake-nappers!"

"Cake-nappers?" cried someone in the crowd who was particularly fond of Ivar's cakes. "How dare they? Get them!"

Vulgar and Freya bounded down the embankment then splashed through the water, racing for the barrel. There was no sign of Knut anywhere.

"Knut?" cried Vulgar. "Knut, where are you?"

There was a loud snore from within the barrel, then a wonky horned helmet appeared above the rim. "Wha—?" muttered Knut. "What's the matter?" He

76

spotted the crowd of angry villagers, who were now plunging into the water right behind Vulgar and Freya. "Ooh, heck," gulped Knut.

"Start rowing, start rowing!" shrieked Vulgar, as he and Freya scrabbled into the barrel.

As they clambered inside, something wet and heavy leapt on to Freya's back. The princess screamed and turned around. "Keep that mutt under control," she snapped, as Grunt dropped down inside the barrel and curled up on the floor.

"He *is* under control," said

77

Vulgar, with a grin. "I told him to do that."

"They're coming!" warned Knut. He wasn't kidding. The edge of the pond had been churned into a foam by the crowd of angry villagers as they gave chase. Ivar was right at the front, hurling abuse and brandishing his rolling pin in a very threatening way.

"Well, start rowing then," barked
Freya. Knut hesitated for a second, then
began madly digging at the water with
the oar.

Slowly, and with a lot of unnecessary
splashing, the barrel-boat began to pull
away from the crowd.

"Thrud's buttocks," said Vulgar. "That
was close!"

"Well?" snapped Freya. Vulgar and
Knut looked at her, blankly. Down
below, Grunt chuffed noisily in his sleep.

"Well what?"

"Did you get them?" asked Freya,
sighing.

A wide grin spread across Vulgar's
face. He rummaged under his tunic and
pulled out four rock cakes. "Of course I
got them."

"All thanks to me," said Freya.

"What? You didn't do anything!"

79

argued Vulgar. "I did all the hard work."

"If it weren't for me, you'd never have got near them," replied Freya.

"Yeah, well, who's the one holding the cakes?" asked Vulgar, waving the cakes in front of her face.

"I am," snapped Freya, snatching two of the cakes away from him.

"Hey, give them back!" cried Vulgar. He tried to take the cakes back, but Freya poked him sharply in the eye.

"No, they're mine," she said, before adding, "Ow!" when Vulgar pulled one of her braids. "You want the cakes?" she shouted. "Have them!"

There was a *clank* as a cake bounced off Vulgar's helmet. It dropped down into the barrel, and was swallowed almost immediately by Grunt.

"No, *you* have them," said Vulgar, hurling one of his cakes at the princess.

She ducked and the cake landed with a *plop* in the water.

"Hey, stop it," said Knut. "You're going to tip us over."

But Vulgar and Freya were too busy fighting to hear what Knut said. Freya kicked Vulgar's shins just as he tried to ram one of the cakes up her delicate royal nose.

The barrel gave a sudden lurch to the side, and dirty pond water spilled inside it. It was up to their knees before Vulgar and Freya noticed what was happening.

"Oh, great," muttered Freya.

"Aegir's toenails, we're going under!" cried Vulgar as the barrel-boat sank, dragging all four of them down with it.

CHAPTER SEVEN

A DAMP DEFEAT

Viking children were not taught many
things, but they were taught how
to swim. Vulgar, Freya and Knut
front-crawled their way through the
murky pond water, with Grunt
doggy-paddling along behind.

Vulgar had dropped the cakes he was
holding, and with every kick he made he
could feel another one falling out
through the leg of his seal-skin shorts.

Ordinary cakes, being light and spongy, may have floated. But not Ivar's rock cakes. They sank to the bottom of the pond, and then, quite probably, sank *through* the bottom of the pond, before coming to a rest somewhere near the Earth's core.

The children and Grunt were shivering with cold and covered from head to toe in slimy green pond scum when they eventually crawled up on to the shore. Several pairs of feet were there to meet them.

The children looked up into the angry faces of a group of villagers. Right at the front stood Ivar, the baker. His eyes blazed as he growled, "Gotcha."

Vulgar looked back at the opposite shore, from where they had just made their daring escape. "But ... but how?" he gasped. "How did you get here so fast?"

"It's a pond, not the North Sea," Ivar told him. "We just walked around it."

"What's going on here?" demanded an angry voice. King Olaf pushed through the crowd, with Harrumf hobbling along behind him.

"'Is Majesticalness wants to know wot's

 85

going on 'ere," said Harrumf. "I suggests someone tells him, right flippin' now."

"Yes, thank you, Harrumf," sighed King Olaf. He stopped right at the front of the crowd, spotted his slime-covered daughter, and almost passed out from the shock. "Freya?" he wheezed. "What's going on?"

"He made me do it," said Freya, pointing an accusing finger at Vulgar. "He kidnapped me and made him help him."

"You little liar!" protested Vulgar. "I didn't even want you to come, but you said I'd go to the dungeon if I didn't let you."

"They were robbing my shop," said Ivar.

"No we weren't," protested Vulgar. "We were pillaging it. There's a big difference."

The next voice that Vulgar heard chilled him to the bone. "You. Did. *WHAT?*"

Vulgar looked up to find his mum glaring down at him. Her eyes were wide open, her mouth was fixed in a snarl, and if he looked closely enough, he was sure he could see steam coming from her ears. He had never seen her so angry.

87

"Hi, Mum," he whimpered, just as a carved wooden face floated on to the shore beside him. "Um, I made you this, look. It's a carving of you."

"He said it would scare sea monsters away," added Freya. She stuck her tongue out at Vulgar as he shot her a dirty look.

"Oh, he did, did he?" growled Vulgar's mum. One of her huge hands clamped down around her son's arm. With a sudden jerk she hoisted him up into the air. "We'll talk about this at home," she said.

"Ha," said Freya. "Serves you right!"

"Not so fast, young lady," said King Olaf. He clapped his hands. "Harrumf," he cried, before realising that Harrumf was standing directly behind him. "Oh, there you are," he said. "Get the princess scrubbed up, then take her to the royal kitchens. I believe she owes Ivar here a new batch of rock cakes."

Vulgar saw Knut edging away from the crowd but unfortunately so did Harrumf.

"Oi, where do you think you're going?" said Harrumf, grabbing Knut by the ear. "You ain't done basket-weaving yet."

Vulgar yelped as his mum slung him over her broad shoulder. He heard Freya and Knut complaining as Helga

89

marched back to
their hut. Vulgar
wondered what fate
awaited him.

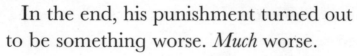

Would his mum
launch him from a
catapult? Tie him
to a whale?
Make him help his
dad clean the village toilets?

In the end, his punishment turned out
to be something worse. *Much* worse.

"A bath?" he wailed. "You can't be
serious! I've already been wet today!"

"Flapping around in mud and pond
scum doesn't count," his mum told him.
She dumped him down next to the basin
in the kitchen. As far as Vulgar could see,
the water in it was even dirtier than the
water in the pond.

"Now, strip off while I go and find that

dog of yours," said Helga. "And don't forget to scrub behind your ears. I'll be checking when I get back."

The door to the hut slammed closed. Vulgar thought about making a run for it, but he knew that would only make things worse. He had to take his punishment, like a real Viking would.

He sighed sadly as he began to peel off his wet clothes. He *wasn't* a proper Viking, though. He had gone off, looting and pillaging, and he had come back empty-handed. Real Vikings never came back empty-handed. They always brought back at least—

There was a *thud* as something heavy rolled out from inside his shorts. Vulgar looked down at the scum-coated lump on the floor, and began to smile.

One cake. Just one. It was soggy and slimy, but it was *there*. He had done it. He had sailed to foreign shores, pillaged their supplies, and returned home, all in the space of an afternoon.

Vulgar slipped into the murky water, took a bite of the rock cake, and sighed happily. Maybe he *would* be a proper Viking, after all.